THE MOON QUILT

SUNNY WARNER

HOUGHTON MIFFLIN COMPANY BOSTON 2001

Walter Lorraine Books

Walter Lorraine (wh) Books

Copyright © 2001 by Sunny Warner
All rights reserved. For information about permission
to reproduce selections from this book, write to
Permissions, Houghton Mifflin Company,
215 Park Avenue South, New York, New York 10003.

Library of Congress Cataloging-in-Publication Data

Warner, Sunny.
  The moon quilt / by Sunny Warner.
    p. cm.
  Summary: With her cat in her lap, an old woman makes a quilt,
  stitching into it the experiences and objects of her life.
  ISBN 0-618-05583-5
  [1. Quilts—Fiction. 2. Cats—Fiction.] I. Title.

PZ7.W24646 Mo 2001
[E]—dc21

00-032007

Printed in Singapore
TWP 10 9 8 7 6 5 4 3 2 1

For my mother, Valedith

It is a day in June, and the old woman is sitting on her porch with her cat. When the old woman's eyes are open, the cat's eyes are closed, and when the old woman's eyes are closed, the cat's eyes are open. Is it because only one needs to look for both to see?

The old woman has fallen asleep. She is dreaming of her old man, who was lost at sea.

She dreams he is sailing in his fishing boat on a
dark rainbow that goes up from the sea to the
moon. Sunlight is slowly spreading from the edge
to the full face of the moon. As he sails toward it,
she sees he is growing younger and younger.

Then she remembers: This is the day to plant pumpkins.
She is planting them so they will be ready for Halloween.
Today the moon is new, and the old woman knows

pumpkin seeds like best to grow when the moon is growing, too. She plants them beside the lilies, the forget-me-nots, and the catnip in her garden.

In the mornings the old woman waters her garden, and at night she sews her quilt.

She has stitched in the rainbow and the fishing boat, and now, with a piece from his shirt, she puts in the old man, young as he was when they met.

Four times the moon wanes and then grows full again. The crickets sing, the fireflies dance, the pumpkins grow, and the old woman sews her quilt.

Now it is
Halloween,
and the
old woman
is rolling
out the
dough for
six pumpkin
pies.
When they
are in the
oven, they
make such a
marvelous
smell that
all the
children she
knows come
knocking at
her door.

The old woman
is glad to see
them, and she
brings them
into her warm
kitchen.

When the children leave, they have eaten all the pies
and they have all cut jack o'lanterns to light their way.

The old woman sits down to finish her quilt. She puts in the children and the pies and the pumpkins. She smiles as she looks at the crickets, the fireflies, the lilies, the forget-me-nots, and the catnip that she has already quilted in.

At last she puts in her black satin cat and herself in her purple velvet dress. When she has stiched the last stitch, her quilt is done.

26

Now it is an evening in November. The old woman is walking in her winter garden with her old cat. The lilies, the forget-me-nots, the fireflies, the crickets, and the pumpkins are gone.

The old woman and the cat sit together under the moon.
They are both glad to rest. The old woman's eyes close,
and in a little while, the cat's eyes close, too.

This is a picture of where they went.